MIRACLE ON SEPARATION STREET

Bob Graham

WALKER
BOOKS

For Caitlin

First published 2010 by Walker Books Ltd
87 Vauxhall Walk, London SE11 5HJ

2 4 6 8 10 9 7 5 3 1

© 2010 Blackbird Design Pty Ltd

The right of Bob Graham to be identified as author
of this work has been asserted by him in accordance
with the Copyright, Designs and Patents Act 1988

This book has been typeset in StempelSchneidler

Printed in Great Britain by Clays Ltd, St Ives plc

British Library Cataloguing in Publication Data:
a catalogue record for this book is available from the British Library

ISBN 978-1-4063-2461-7

CONTENTS

MIRACLES

There! I've started it. Well, I've written the
name of the story, so that has to be a start.
I've found this exercise book left over from
school last year and ripped out the pages
at the front with sums on. So I have the
rest of the book to say what happened.

Here's my idea. I'm going to write this
story, and when I'm finished, I'm going
to put it in a biscuit tin with some bubble
wrap around it and then plant it in the yard
downstairs. You know? Like those time

capsules where they stick things in that might be interesting to someone in the future. A bus ticket, or a newspaper, or the football results – just ordinary stuff. So in about five hundred years there might be this team of people scratching away in the dirt with paint scrapers like they do on TV, and one might say, "Look at this. This is a pretty interesting kid." And they would read through my story and the rest of the things I put in there and get to the football results and say,

"Those East Side Rangers were a pretty hopeless side. They didn't win a match." (The Rangers happen to be *our* local team.)

I might put just my story in the biscuit tin rather than all the other stuff. Or not, depending on how I feel.

Now I see the name of my story, I realize that what happened wasn't really a *miracle*, not like when those kids in France saw the Virgin Mary looking at them, so now grown-ups keep coming back to the spot to see if they can see her too. No, it wasn't like that.

It was just that my mum said it was a miracle and, well, occasionally you have to take notice of my mum; she can say things that are quite true – sometimes *really* true. Sometimes she seems to know what I'm thinking, like she's got X-ray vision into my head.

Like, every so often we see this bent old lady with long grey hair, and she looks pretty poor and pushes all her stuff around in a shopping trolley. She seems to spend all day walking around with nothing to do and nowhere to go.

Mum heard me say once how sad and ancient she looked, which started her off on one of her quotes. It goes (with her finger wagging a bit):

"When all the world is young, lad,
And all the trees are green…"

And the poem rabbits on and then it goes:

"When all the world is old, lad,
And all the trees are brown…"

And something about *"all the wheels run down"*, then *"Creep home, and take your place there"*.

It gets to that bit and that does for me – it's a real downer and makes me feel pretty miserable and bad for calling someone old; but at the same time it's pretty wise, if you know what I mean (even if it's someone

10

else's poem, and my mum hasn't written it).

So what I'm about to tell you could have been a miracle, but I guess it depends on what you think is a miracle.

Mum's always telling me, "Jack, don't keep saying things are *brilliant* or *amazing* or *gross*, because they aren't." She says, "Those words are just too much; you've got nowhere to go after you use them." I'm never really sure what she means by that. All I know is that it was *her* – my mum, I mean – who came up with the word *miracle* at the time, which seemed pretty extreme to me, but there you are. That's what I'm calling my story.

The Separation Street bit is true, because that's where we live; and so is the story, because it happened to us a few years ago – our family, I mean. That's my mum, my dad, my little brother (Duggie) and me – not counting Madam Brown, the guinea pig.

It was all to do with cars. Well, no.
I should say it was all to do with us not
having one. We went everywhere on foot,
or Mum took that old pram with Duggie
and Madam Brown inside it, and I was
always really embarrassed when they came
to pick me up from school.

Most of the other parents had these big cars, and they would drive around in them and say to my mum, "You're lucky not having a car *really*. They're so expensive. More trouble than they're worth." And then they would zoom off. And the word *really* used to annoy my mum for some reason.

Don't get me wrong; we were pretty happy. We did things on the weekend, and sometimes my mate Sam came along. Sam's OK. He lives over on Arcadia Avenue, which has big houses and lots of trees. He's got a dad I've hardly ever seen, a mum with a red spot right in the middle of her forehead who's also at work a lot – oh, and he's got Space Freaks II, which we sometimes play until our thumbs hurt, and a really big trampoline in his back garden.

Yes, Sam's all right and he seems to like it at our place more than his. I don't know why, because ours is so much smaller. I think he likes my mum, and most of the time, as much as adults can be, she's really fun. She bakes us fairy cakes with heaps of cream on and

14

plays wild games and makes Sam laugh a lot. But sometimes when it's raining and we're all cooped up together and us kids are busting to get out and there's all this energy building up in our flat and Dad's not home from work yet, I can see that Mum's getting pretty strung out with it all. Not that she ever *shows* it much, but I can tell; I can see ... me, Jack, with my Special Powers. It might be something like a long strand of hair starting to hang over her face, but she doesn't brush it back with her hand. She blows it away through the corner of her mouth and the hair just dances round a bit. Then I know she's getting edgy. Adults think you don't notice these things, but you do.

So that's
when we bust
out of there (even if
it's raining a bit) into the
courtyard and bang around
with the ball or something
until the Angry Lady in the flat
upstairs lifts up her window and tells
us to be quiet. It's dumb, she's telling us to
keep quiet but I bet she can hardly hear us
over the noise of all the big trucks and traffic
and stuff going past.

I bet she wouldn't order the Mob to be
quiet, but I'll tell you about them in a minute
because now I need to get on with
my story.

That's me, really. When I begin to explain things, I get sidetracked. My dad says, "Jack, you start out on the motorway and you finish up on a tiny one-way country lane."

Anyway, what was I saying? Oh yes, I've got to tell you about the Wall. I love going there; I could hang out there all day if I was old enough to go on my own. Sometimes on Saturday mornings my dad would say, "Let's go see Decco surfing the Wall."

I would say, "Don't bring the pram, Mum. Madam Brown can stay at home."

"Oh, sad!" Mum often said. "I'll put her in my handbag instead."

Dad would lift Duggie onto his shoulders, and Duggie would be up there looking down on all these white spots in Dad's hair left over from yesterday's work (Dad helps a bloke paint houses). So picture this: along with the spots, Dad's jumper or shirt is also covered with all these little bits of white tissue left over from the washing machine and he'd look like he'd been walking in the snow.

We would collect Sam from his house and walk to the town hall, and this really tough-looking older kid in a hood would be there hanging out with these other kids. And they'd all be really cool, some doing little flipping movements with their skateboards. Suddenly there'd be Decco (the tough-looking one) flipping up onto this stone wall and racing along the top like he was on a wave, and he'd go flying off the end and drop about two metres onto the pavement with this great CRASH!

And there'd be people looking round
wondering what was going on and he'd
just walk away all casual like nothing had
happened. I don't care what Mum says,
I call that *extreme*!

Sam and I got the idea a long time ago
that it was very uncool even to show you
were looking. But my mum and dad never
did get it. They'd clap and whistle.
It was embarrassing.

One time when they did that, Decco (you couldn't see his eyes back there under his hood) just stood there and stared at them for what seemed ages, and I was getting pretty uneasy. Then he nodded.

You could hardly see his hood move, but he definitely nodded.

How cool was that? I think *that* was some kind of miracle.

Other times Sam and
I just hung around the flats
with our own skateboards. Once, Dad
made us a ramp out of wood and we lined
up six of Duggie's cars in front of it and tried
to jump over them.

Sam landed right on top and dented
Duggie's London bus, and one of the wheels
came off and he was not at all pleased. In
fact he yelled so loud that he stopped the
Mob mid-game.

Now, if you don't know the Mob, they
can seem pretty scary. Certainly the Angry

Lady never sticks her head out of the window and tells *them* to stop playing ball in the courtyard, like she does with us. I mean, some people say the Mob are responsible for all the writing on the walls, but I've never seen them. What I *did* see, though, was that Duggie's name had been added to the graffiti on the wall. It said *Duggie Rocks!* and I know it wasn't Duggie; he was too young. It probably *was* the Mob, because they are pretty keen on Duggie, and I remember when it started.

This was all a few years back, as I said, and Duggie was a tiny little kid. He'd always had trouble saying his "r"s, but he got a bit better, although they sometimes came out as "w"s. But he still couldn't say his "l"s at all. His tongue just wouldn't do it. So one morning, Duggie was watching the Mob play basketball in the courtyard and he just walked up to them – he's a pretty brave

little kid – and they
stopped playing
and he looked at
them and said,
"Can I pray
with you?"
Sam and I
were watching,
and Sam
smacked
his hand
over his
mouth and
whispered,
"Oh, no!" And it all went quiet.
The Mob, they looked at each other – and
to be fair, they didn't make fun of him or
burst out laughing or anything like that,
although they were raising their eyebrows
and trying not to smile. The big one, he said,
"I think this cat wants to *play* with us."

And they did. Played with
Duggie, I mean, and you
could see they were all
pretty chuffed by him.
I would have given
anything for them even
to notice me, and here
they were including
Duggie in their game.
I wouldn't use the
word *jealous*, but let
me say this: I would
have loved to be there
instead of Duggie,
doing that stuff with
the ball.

So after that they
all treated him as if
he was some kind of
mascot – you know, like
when football teams

have a little kid who runs out in front of the team to start the game, like he or she is good luck or something.

There's one called the Human Tower, or Tower for short, or shorter still they call him Tow (that rhymes with *how* or *cow*). He's so tall, he can just drop the ball down into the basket. "Yo, man! What's up wit' ya?" he'll say. Once, he lifted Duggie right up and sat him on the ring and Duggie perched there for a minute, saw Tower with his big hands stretched wide so he wouldn't fall, and then he burst out laughing.

That's the sort of stuff we did without a car.

Then Mum got it into her head (and I'm talking a few years back here), she had this idea that we could get away a bit, have fun on the weekend, if we had a car.

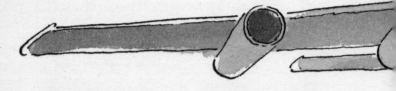

She said even if it was raining, *especially* if it was raining, we could bust out of our flat and drive somewhere interesting that we couldn't get to by train or bus.

I'd heard at school about this place out on the far side of the airport where all these people go with their cars, and some even take a picnic. They stop by the side of the road and watch the planes taking off one after the other and they come over this spot ... almost on top of your head. You can't

hear yourself
think and your
head is going to
be knocked off
any minute, and
all the while people
are just standing there
sipping tea out of their
Thermos flasks. WICKED!!!

Of course, we all agreed with her. "Get the car! Get the car!" we yelled – everyone except Dad. He wasn't so sure and asked, "Can we afford this, Kate?" My mum said that she had a bit of money put away and she would work for the rest. And then we could get it.

You have to hand it to my mum – when she wants to do something, there's no stopping her, even if she's just making a chocolate cake (and we don't try and stop her doing that anyway). It might be going all wrong in the kitchen (sometimes it does), but she just keeps on until it's right. When she comes out, she might have a whole lot of chocolate over her where it shouldn't be. But she has done it. She *perseveres*, I think that's what it's called. So she had this idea and then she did it – got a job, I mean.

It was at our local store, the Corner Emporium, and she mopped the floor and stuff at night when it was all closed up, and we used to go down there and look through the window, then take her in a cup of tea, and this went on for months and we got to going in and Dad did some mopping and mum worked that scrubby polisher thing that gets out of control and Duggie sat up on top and sometimes we didn't help at all and we had to leave anyway for Duggie and me to go to bed.

(I suppose I should have put a full stop in there somewhere but it doesn't matter because it's not a school thing and I'm not going to get a mark or anything like that for it. It's just for me in my own book at home. And maybe for the biscuit tin.)

Anyway, what I was saying was that we visited Mum at work for ages, until Duggie and me eventually got sick of going down there, because Mum wouldn't let us have anything out of the Slush Shlime drinks machine. She said she didn't want us going to bed "all sugared up" as she called it.

So to cut a long story short (even though I've got loads of pages left in this book), she finished the night job and came home and said...

"Right! CAR!"

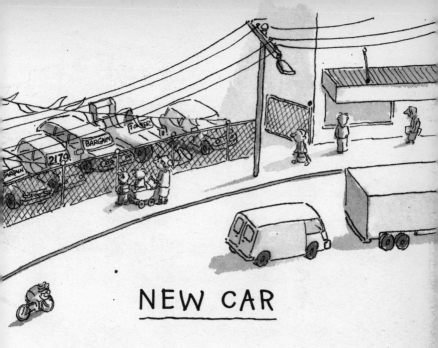

NEW CAR

Next day after school, me, Mum and
Duggie, along with Madam Brown, walked
home down Separation Street, as we
always do.

I don't know why they call it Separation
Street, because I can't see it separates
anything from anything else. It looks pretty
much the same on both sides to me. Except
that on one side, on the way home from
school, there is a used car yard called Flash
Motors with bright fluoro plastic flags

hanging over it like they're about to have
a big party inside or something.

Mum was pushing the old pram, because
she always wants to get Madam Brown out
in the afternoons. "Keeps her interested,"
Mum says, but as usual it was pretty
embarrassing. So she had Madam Brown in
there along with Duggie and some shopping.

I wish she wouldn't do it –
bring the pram to school,
I mean. She says to
me, "Jack, you
worry too
much about
what people
think." And
it's true, I do.
Duggie, he doesn't
seem to worry about anything. He sits up on
top of Madam Brown's cage like he's captain
of a ship.

What was I saying? Oh yes, Mum pushed
the pram into Flash Motors on Separation
and there was this man standing by the cars
wearing a really neat suit and a tie with little
shields over it, the sort knights carried in the
olden days. He said, "You want a trade-in
on that, do you?" and nodded at the pram in
a jokey way. A trade-in is when you swap
something for something else so you don't
have to pay so much for it.

My mum smiled and said,

"No, but I want a car big enough to
put it in the back along with a husband,
two kids, a friend and a guinea pig – oh!
And *me*."

So we came away about two seconds
later with a new car – or an old car, I
suppose. Well, it wasn't two seconds, but
I don't think the bloke selling the cars
could believe it. He and Mum signed some
papers in the office and the salesman hardly

had time to scrape the price off
the windscreen before we were away.
I'd wanted Mum to buy the big red zippy
one, but she said it only had one seat and
… what else did she say? She said she
wanted the one where "you could get a
horse in the back". Well, you couldn't have
done *that*, but it sure had a lot of space to fit
everything else in, including the pram, and
it had a little seat specially for Duggie. The
people who'd owned it (and it was beaten
around a bit) must have had a little kid
about Duggie's age.

Mum buckled Duggie and me into our seats, which had this very sweet clean smell. "It smells like we're sitting in the middle of a pine forest," said Mum, acting all kind of cool as she checked out the various buttons and knobs. But her hands were shaking a bit, I think with excitement. The car was really

old-fashioned, because it only had a tape player, and I found an old tape still in the glove box called *Uncle Earl and His Mountain Mud Stompers*.

Mum put it in the slot and on the way home we had Uncle Earl singing and Mum singing and in the background a mouth organ that sounded like a runaway steam train. Only we weren't going anywhere. We were stuck in the traffic.

When we finally got home, we parked
in front of the flats with "Banjo-Picker's
Breakdown" bouncing off the walls.
Mum turned off the engine and everything
suddenly went very quiet – even the traffic
in the street. She called over to the Mob,
"Hey, boys, come and have a look at our
new car."

You have to know this about my mum: she has no fear. We might be sitting on a train, right? Imagine this. We get on a carriage which has seats where you can be by yourself and seats facing each other. And on one of the facing seats is a bloke covered with tats of skulls and blood and stuff and with all these sharp things sticking out of him, through his lips and nose and eyebrow, with a bad-looking little spike under his lip. So which seat does my mum choose?

Guess.

Correct! She chooses the one not even opposite but *right next to* him. He's sitting there looking like a really bad, mean pirate. He might as well have a neon sign blinking across his forehead: KEEP OUT. DANGER. NO TRESPASSING.

Now what does she do? She starts chatting to him. All he does is kind of grunt, but she keeps going, and somehow, before we get off, he gives this louder than usual grunt. Which I think is a laugh.

My mum knows no fear.

I'm glad I'm not writing this for school or anything like that. My teacher would probably say (like she does when I write my stories), "Jack, you're getting all your tenses mixed up."

There's present tense, which is Now (why don't they just say that?), and there's past tense, which is Then, like Before. So I'm writing this Now, about Before, and coming back to Now. My teacher would say, "Jack, you're swapping between present tense and past tense like there's no tomorrow."

So, back to the story. The Mob came over all cool and loose, saying, "Yo! Check it out, bro!" and slowly bouncing their ball as they walked, and the Human Tower hoisted Duggie onto his shoulders and they all peered under the bonnet like they knew what they were looking at, and I bet they did too. Then they got Mum to switch on the engine and Tower put Duggie gently down, then sort of uncurled himself like a big praying mantis, put his giant, big-as-a-baseball-glove hand in and tugged something. It made the engine go like crazy and as loud as a chainsaw

with blue smoke coming up, like the start
of one of those Formula One races.

Tow slowly straightened up,
kicked the tyre and said,
"Top motor."

How cool was that?

I could see that Mum felt pretty proud.
She said, "Oh! Thank you…" Then she
paused and added in a smaller voice,
"Tower." Like she was putting her toe gently
in the water and watching the ripples spread
out. "Is Tower all right?
Is that what your
mum calls you?"

He looked
down at my mum,
spun the basketball
on one finger and
said, "You got
it, man!"

When Dad saw the car, he didn't kick the tyre or even look at the engine. He put his arms around Mum. "You *did* it! You worked hard all winter and you earned that car. And it's lovely. It's got your name all over it."

Then he hugged Mum some more and looked a bit emotional. Well, of course it didn't have her name all over it, but I knew what he meant. Mum and that car were made for each other.

Then he added, "You didn't buy it at Flash Motors, did you?" Mum nodded. "Not off that bloke with the little moustache and the oily hair?"

My mum nodded again and said quickly, "He looked a nice man, and he was too."

End of story for my mum, and Dad knew the questions were over. He gave her a kiss and looked at the big space in the back of the car. "We could get Madam Brown in there," he said.

"And a football team."

Well, you couldn't get the East Side Rangers in there, the same as you couldn't get a horse. But mums and dads exaggerate like that sometimes. And they tell me not to!

Now I'm getting on with my story, because this is where it really starts. When we got the car, I mean. I'll write some more tomorrow.

* * *

Tomorrow

The next night, Mum was acting all funny. She told us to put our pyjamas on but I no way wanted to, and neither did Duggie.

"Mum, you have to be joking. We don't ever do this till well after dinner," I said.

"Well, this is different," she said. "We're going to the drive-in movies in our new car."

I asked what drive-in movies were and my dad said, "It's like in the olden days. They would have this huge screen outside and you would sit in your car along with lots of other cars and watch a film, with a speaker for the sound hanging inside the car window."

Mum added, "And you could buy fish and chips or a hamburger and eat it in the car while you were watching the film. And you still *can*."

"UNREAL!" I yelled, and even Duggie

was waving his arms around, although I don't think he really understood.

So anyway, we got into our pyjamas early and we drove for ages out to the edge of the city somewhere to The Last Drive-In Cinema, with Dad trying to figure out how the tape player worked all the while.

"You're trying to put it in back to front, Dad," I said.

"Oh!" was all he managed, then there was a satisfying CLUNK! and a hissing sound and we had Uncle Earl back with us.

We got there and parked beside a load of other cars, hooked the speaker to the window, and Dad said, "Hamburger, anyone?"

"YE-E-E-SS!" we yelled as the windows started to fog up. Dad went by himself. (Who would want to be seen in Hamburger Heaven in their pyjamas? Not me.)

We ate our burger and chips in the car, and Duggie dropped half of his down the back of the seat. The film wasn't really suitable for him, but he went to sleep anyway. There was a really old-fashioned lady in it with her hair in little rings, and her face all white like it had flour all over it. And there was this man on a camel who seemed to make her short of breath and her eyes flutter a lot. And love stuff. Boring! Or maybe boringly interesting (but as no one will read this for five hundred years I can secretly say it was fun, just to be there and eating hamburgers and doing it).

On the way home… Shall I go into it? I may as well, because there are a lot more pages left, and some people in the future might find little things like this interesting. On the way back we had this strange conversation about whether the car was male or female, a boy or a girl, because

Mum wanted to give it a name. It wasn't till we were waiting at the traffic lights near home that Dad said, "Well, I think your mum should have the final say. It's her who has worked all this time to buy her – or should I say 'him'?"

Mum put the car in gear and it leapfrogged forward, making our heads nod on our shoulders. "Sorry," she said, "still getting used to her."

"That's it, then," I said. "It's a her."

"Yep," replied Mum. "It's a girl, and her name is … Maybeline. Or May Belle – or maybe May for short."

When we got out of the car, Dad carried Duggie up the stairs and I saw Mum stop, go back three steps and rub a squashed bug off the bonnet with her finger. Then she polished the spot with the sleeve of her shirt. Seeing those little things sometimes breaks me up.

So all of us went to bed very late. I just lay
there for a long time and imagined the car
standing on its spot on the concrete, cooling
down and probably not smelling of a pine
forest any more, but of Duggie's hamburger
and chips down the back of the seat.

I'll have to finish this bit later, because
I'm due to meet Sam soon to muck about a
bit. He has so much stuff, Sam. He's got a
proper football like they use in the FA Cup
and he thinks he can keep it in the air for
one minute without using his hands. But
I've never seen him.

Later

Sam didn't keep the ball in the air for a minute. I borrowed his watch and timed him. Twenty-three seconds, though. Pretty good, I must say.

So now I have to tell you the next part, which is not good. I just hate it when things are too sad for someone – when things don't turn out well for them. Like that bent lady with the shopping trolley. My dad feels the same as I do. He can't bear for people to be let down. So if you're really looking forward to something, he might say, "Well, don't get *too* worked up, just in case it doesn't happen."

Here comes the bad bit. It was like that for my mum.

The morning after we went to the drive-in, she was pretty excited. "I'll drive you to school today," she said, and went on making the Vegemite sandwiches, but I could tell she was really pumped up about turning up with me and Duggie and Madam Brown in the back instead of pushing the old pram like usual.

So we came out onto the concrete parking area and she was saying, "Better leave plenty of time for the traffic," and we got to our spot …

... and the car was gone.

CAR-LESS

I wrote it small because I feel like I only
want to whisper it, even now, even after a
few years. Mum just stood there and looked
at where she had left the car. All that was
left was an oil spot where it had stood. Then
she looked round the corner, maybe thinking
she had left it somewhere else.

Then she sort of … crumpled!

"Someone's … someone's … stolen our car." Her voice went all shaky and she burst into tears.

I'd never seen my mum cry, not really. Sometimes she might get a tiny bit teary, but never like this. I tried to be strong but my lip went all quivery and Duggie burst into tears and then I followed. I'll say it: I was sad as much for Mum as about the car.

Then Dad appeared. "Kate, Kate, I don't know what to say," he said. "All that work, you *worked* for that car. You…"

Then he started to tear up himself. Mum gave this kind of brave smile and shook her head and did little wavy fanning motions with her hands in front of her face, like trying to dry up her tears, and said, "Well, boys, we're back to walking to school."

So out came the pram again.

Dad went to work, we walked to school, then we walked home again in the afternoon with the cars speeding past, blowing Mum's hair about as we pushed the pram together. It was like nothing had ever happened. It was like we'd never had a car at all.

Mum had nothing, like, wise to say about it, no poems to quote or anything like that. Maybe no one has written a Stolen Car poem.

All she said when I mentioned it was, "It's not important, Jack."

But it was important to me, because for the next few days there was this feeling around that the world was mean, that everyone was out to get you. The trouble was that I started looking at everyone like it could have been them who'd driven off with Uncle Earl singing, and them breathing in the smell of Duggie's burger and chips bought specially on our drive-in night.

Dad started looking sideways at the Mob like they might have done it, and that didn't help Mum at all.

What did help was when Tower called out to her, as his ball whacked down through the basket, "Sorry to hear about your motor, man!" (they called everyone *man*, even if they happened to be your mum) and another one, called the Priest, said, "See what we can hear on the street." Then Tower said, "We'll check out the Crick," which I think meant they would

look down at
Stringy Bark
Creek, where there
were no stringy
bark trees any more,
only rusty shopping
trolleys.

I suppose they meant that someone might have just pushed it down the bank when they were finished with it and left it sitting in the water. I couldn't even think about that.

My mum said, "Thanks, boys," and gave another of her brave smiles.

We had to go to the police station, but the policeman didn't look too upset. "Happens all the time," he said. "They'll take anything around here. Anything that isn't bolted down. Someone lost his boots off the front doorstep last week." He peered down at Duggie's feet. "*You* didn't take them, did you, young fella?"

Duggie's lip started to quiver. "Sorry, just a joke," said the policeman. And he patted Duggie on the head and said, "We'll be in touch if we find it. And I say IF."

My dad said the car wasn't *assured* – or was it *insured*? Whatever the word is, it's like you pay all this money to someone and they'll give you some back one day if you bash up your car, or someone steals it or something. Sounds like a pretty dumb idea to me. Anyway, my mum wasn't assured so she wasn't going to get her money back.

On top of that – when was that? The Wednesday, I think – on the Saturday, when we went up to the town hall to watch Decco and his gang, then it was *me* looking at them and thinking that maybe it was them who had run away with our car.

So there was Dad thinking it was probably the Mob, and now it was me thinking it might be Decco and the skateboard riders, and there was a bad feeling like we were in the middle of this big dark cloud and looking at people like they were all capable of pinching stuff.

But my mum only said, "Why would they steal our car? Because of the way they look?"

"Well, you worked hard for it, Kate, and *someone* took it," said Dad.

My mum shot a glance over at my dad (pretty cross, I think she was), then she kind of relaxed,

scuffed the toe of her boot around a
bit, then said, "Well, I hope they
like *Uncle Earl and His Mountain
Mud Stompers*."

That was all my mum said.
She didn't say it might be
someone in particular
who stole Maybeline,
but then she wouldn't.
My mum only ever sees
the best in people.

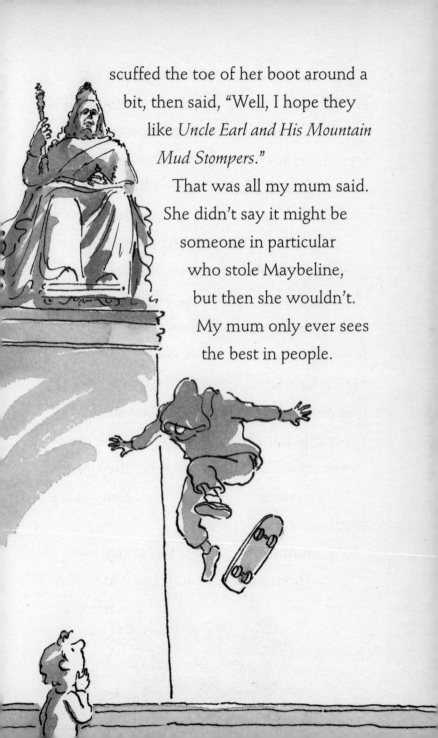

The Angry Lady
found out; she knows
about everything. She
leant her elbows on the
windowsill. "Around
here," she said, "even if
you bolted your car to
the ground you'd lose
it. You should padlock
your doors. Be on
your guard. Children
have no respect.
No manners. Speak
dreadfully. Don't stand
up for you on trains.

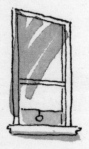

Not like when I was young." Et cetera, et cetera. (That *et cetera, et cetera* means she went on a lot more like this.)

So what did my mum say when the Angry Lady was finished? She just said, "I don't find that at all, Francesca."

That's it, and she walked away.

At home she said to me, "Francesca. She started her life with such a beautiful name. Now she's so angry."

I have to admit that deep down inside *I* was angry too. I didn't know what I should be feeling. I think I should have been more angry for my mum losing her car like that, but I was angry for *me*, because I would never get to see the planes take off. So that made me feel bad.

Now I'm writing about it, it makes me want to finish – but there's more to come and I still haven't explained the miracle bit. I'll try and get to that tomorrow.

Tomorrow

Well, tomorrow turns out to be really today, because that's when I'm writing this now … today! Present tense. No, correction, it happened a few years back. Ages ago, in fact. Past tense!

On Sunday mornings we were (still are) allowed to watch the old cartoons on TV. On this particular Sunday Duggie was sitting on my back and we were watching a mouse flatten a cat with a frying pan.

The cat's face took
the shape of the pan
before it bounced back
as his old face again.
Then the little guy,
now being chased by
the cat, ran out over this
massively high cliff.
AND HE DIDN'T KNOW!
He just kept running –
until he saw he was up in
the clouds. Then he fell
into the canyon, about
three thousand feet below.
And he was OK again!

I always love that about cartoons. It's nice to think that mice can win by being smarter than big bully cats. Cartoons make everything all right again.

"I'm just popping down to the Corner Emporium to get the Sunday papers and some milk," Mum called, "then I'll make you pancakes as a special treat."

I said I'd come with her, because Duggie was still in his pyjamas and he's really hard

to get out of them sometimes; he puts on a
big show, like crying and going all red in the
face and curling up his fists. He's a funny kid.

So, what I'm saying is that I went with
Mum and left Duggie with Dad. That
cartoon made me feel like, well, happy and
hopeful again.

Anyway, we were crossing the courtyard,
and (I'm even feeling strange now as I'm
telling you this) … Mum suddenly stopped.

AND THE CAR
WAS BACK!

Smack bang right where we'd left it! And Mum's hands flew up to her face and her mouth made a perfect O but nothing came out.

Then she walked forward very slowly like she couldn't believe what she was seeing and thought that when she got there she'd be able to put her hand straight through the image of the car like it was some sort of ghost. Or that somehow she might have imagined or dreamt that the car had gone missing and it had actually been there all the time.

This next bit is true and I'm not making it up ... OK? We got right up close, and on the bonnet was a bunch of flowers all tied together with string.

They weren't like those really posh ones you buy in the shops or anything like that; they were flowers that might have come out of someone's garden, with some weedy ones in there too.

Mum just stood there turning the bunch of flowers round and round in her hands, looking at them like they were the first flowers she had ever seen, and saying, "Oh, my! Oh, my! Oh, my!"

Under the windscreen wiper was a bit of paper and Mum unfolded it and read aloud:

Sorry about that. I live right out on the edge of the city and it was really late and I didn't have my train fare ... and it seemed a good idea at the time. I always meant to bring it back.
Sorry it's taken a few days.

All my mum said was, "It's a miracle."

That's it, really. I mean, what was I saying earlier? I don't reckon it was a miracle. I reckon a miracle would be if East Side Rangers ever scores a goal this season against anybody.

Just joking.

So, what happened next? Well, Mum looked at the flowers some more and smelt them a bit, then read the note again and had a cry. Not a big one like before, but another kind.

Now

To bring you right up to date, well, we still walk
to school most days. We still sometimes see
Decco and his mates, but the people in the
town hall have stuck metal bits along the top
of the Wall so Decco can't do his surfing stunts
any more. How mean is that?

But what they do now is skateboard down
the town hall steps. They all go up to the top,
as cool as ever, and some make a giant leap
down the steps on their boards – but Decco,
he doesn't go down the steps; he goes
DOWN THE HANDRAIL. He hits
the pavement at the bottom
at about 300 K an hour,
and there's pigeons
going everywhere, and
he does this kind of
back turn, his board
flips into the air
and he catches it.

I mean, my mum says not to say *extreme* and stuff, but she says *miracle* so I can say *mega extreme*.

Oh, there's a couple more surprising bits that I can put in. Things that happened afterwards.

First I heard that Decco and his mates had collected all these old skateboards and painted them and got the wheels like new, and then they sent them off to some place where the kids are really poor and don't have anything to do.

And sometimes bombs and things are going off there and it's really dangerous and the kids have learnt how to do tricks and all the moves and are getting really good on the boards, and in the middle of all that, the bombs and all, the government over there is trying to stop them skating in the town square.

I know I should have more full stops, so here's another one. ←

Right, then. The other bit is about that old lady, the one with the shopping trolley, who I felt sorry for. Well, we were walking through this really posh department store and they had a huge black grand piano, right in the middle of the make-up department. What do they call it? Cosmetics.

And there was the old lady, her trolley full of all her stuff parked next to the lipsticks, and she was sitting at the piano with her back really straight and she was playing this beautiful music. One minute it was simple and soft, then it was loud like a whole waterfall of notes tumbling over one another to get to the bottom, and

people were stopping and trying to leave
her money. But she shook her head because
she just wanted to sit there and play.

Sometimes people really surprise you.
Things don't happen like you might expect.

85

Can't think of much else. Oh, the Mob bought Duggie a proper regulation little basketball just the same as theirs only smaller. And although he can now say his "r"s pretty much all the time, his question has become legend with the Mob. Tow, who now plays with the East Side All Saints, says, "Come and pray with us, Duggie?" And Duggie is doing some pretty good moves down there on the concrete.

We drive out to the beach a lot on Sundays, and sometimes Sam comes too. We sit on the sand and have a picnic with all the seagulls wanting a bit of Vegemite sandwich or curry puff that Sam's mum sends along.

Duggie always comes home sopping wet and he brings heaps of stuff back with him,

like shells, old crab claws and bits of dry
seaweed that often fall out of his pocket or
his fist when he goes to sleep and straight
down the back of the seat to join his old
chips and hamburger, which must be pretty
mummified by now. So our car doesn't smell
of a pine forest any more. Probably more
like low tide at the beach.

I wanted Mum to get a new CD player
for the car, but she said she's happy with
the old tape player. So now we have to
go to those charity shops – you know, the
ones where all the clothes are hanging up
and smell of mothballs – to look for tapes
to play in our car, and all that Mum can
find are really dumb ones like *The Victor
Lightfoot Dance Band Plays Light Operetta.*

Apart from the car coming back, here is
the best thing, which I've left till last.

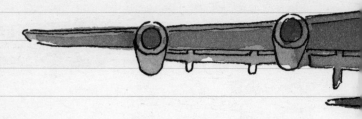

About two weeks after we got the car back,
we drove out to the edge of the airport.
We all got out and held on to the fence,
our knuckles white as this plane came
STRAIGHT TOWARDS US.

"Hands over ears!" yelled Dad as Duggie
did a little shuffling dance of excitement. It
pretty much made a parting in Dad's hair as
it howled over us, the wind whipping the little
pieces of white tissue off his jumper and
making them dance in the air. And the planes
kept coming like big waves over the horizon.

88

Mum yelled, "They're as
big and heavy as our block of
flats. How do they stay in the air?"

If you ask me, I would say THAT'S
a miracle.

In the end I didn't put my story in a biscuit tin and plant it. I stuck it in the back of a drawer and have just found it. That's why I'm adding this recent bit. As I said, it happened a fair while ago now. But even if you pin Mum down and threaten to tickle her unless she says it wasn't, she still says it WAS.

A miracle, I mean.

"Come for a swim in our pool," said Dampsy. "The day gets better as we all get wetter!"

Daisy and her animal friends are on a woodland expedition to find and photograph some rather shy otters. But somewhere in the treetops birds are singing songs about storms — will Daisy get her picture before the bad weather gets them?

BEL MOONEY

Best Dog
Bonnie

The little dog with big ideas

"There's a dog show soon," said Mum. "Let's turn Bonnie into a champion dog!"

Before you can say "Crufts" or Harry can groan "Oh no", Bonnie is whisked down to the Millionhairs Dog Grooming Parlour to be buffed and bouffed to perfection.

But Bonnie isn't just a pretty face, and this little dog has her own ideas about being Best in Show.

BOB GRAHAM is one of
Australia's finest author-illustrators.
Winner of the Kate Greenaway Medal,
Smarties Book Prize and CBCA Picture
Book of the Year, he is renowned for
celebrating in his stories the magic of
everydayness. Bob says, "I'd like reading
my books to be a little like opening a
family photo album, glimpsing small
moments captured from daily lives."
His books include *Queenie the Bantam*,
"Let's Get a Pup!", *Max*, *Jethro Byrde,
Fairy Child* and a younger story about
Jack and his family, *Jack's Little Party*.
Bob lives in Melbourne, Australia, with
his wife. They have two grandchildren –
who call him "Bob" and not "Grandad"
because he doesn't feel ready for
slippers or rocking chairs just yet.